Alligator Baby

Robert Munsch

Illustrated by
Michael Martchenko

Cartwheel
B·O·O·K·S®

SCHOLASTIC INC.
New York Toronto London Auckland Sydney

To Kristen Bocking, Guelph, Ontario.

— R.M.

Illustrations in this book were painted in watercolor
on Crescent Illustration Board.

This book was designed in QuarkXPress,
with type set in 18 point Hiroshige Medium.

ISBN 0-590-88594-4

Text copyright © 1997 by Bob Munsch Enterprises, Ltd.
Illustrations copyright © 1997 by Michael Martchenko.
All rights reserved. Published by Scholastic Inc., 555 Broadway, New York, NY 10012, by arrangement with Scholastic Canada, Ltd.

12 11 10 9 8 7 6 5 4 3 2 1   8 9/9 0/0 01 02

Printed in the U.S.A.   24

First Scholastic trade paperback printing, September 1998

One night Kristen's mother woke up and yelled, "A baby! A baby! I'm having a baby!"

Kristen's father jumped up, zoomed around the room, got dressed, and grabbed Kristen's mother by the hand. They ran downstairs to the car and drove off really fast.

Varoooooooooommmm.

Unfortunately, they got lost. They didn't go to the hospital, they went to the zoo. But it was okay. Kristen's mother had a lovely baby. Then they drove home and knocked on their front door: *blam, blam, blam, blam, blam*.

Kristen opened the door and there was her mother, holding something all wrapped up.

"Kristen," she said, "would you like to see your new baby brother?"

"Oh, yes," said Kristen.

So Kristen lifted up the bottom of the blanket. She saw a long green tail and said, "That's not a people tail."

Kristen lifted up the middle of the blanket, saw a green claw, and said, "That's not a people claw."

Kristen lifted up the top of the blanket, saw a long green face with lots of teeth, and said, "That's not a people face! That is *not* my baby brother!"

"Now, Kristen," said her mother, "don't be jealous."

4

Just then the baby reached up and bit Kristen's mother on the nose. She yelled, *"Aaaaaahhhhhaaaaa!"*

Then the baby reached up and bit her father on the nose. He yelled, *"Aaaaaahhhhhaaaaa!"*

"That's not a people baby," said Kristen. "That's an alligator baby."

"Goodness," said her mother. "We've got the wrong baby!"

So Kristen put the alligator baby into the fish tank, and her mother and father drove back to the zoo. They came back in an hour and knocked on the door: *blam, blam, blam, blam, blam.*

Kristen opened the door and her mother said, "Would you like to see your new baby brother?"

"Oh, yes," said Kristen.

Kristen lifted up the bottom of the blanket, saw a fishy tail, and said, "That's not a people tail."

Kristen lifted up the middle of the blanket, saw a flipper, and said, "That's not a people flipper."

Kristen lifted up the top of the blanket, saw a face with whiskers, and said, "That's not a people face. That is *not* my baby brother!"

"Now, Kristen," said her mother, "don't be jealous."

Just then the baby reached up with its flipper and flapped her father's face: *wap, wap, wap, wap, wap, wap, wap.*

He yelled, *"Aaaaaahhhhhaaaaa!* It's a seal baby! We've got the wrong baby."

So Kristen put the seal baby in the bathtub, and her mother and father drove back to the zoo.

They came back in an hour and knocked on the door: *blam, blam, blam, blam, blam.* They said, "Kristen, would you like to see your new baby brother?"

"Oh, yes," said Kristen.

She lifted up the bottom of the blanket, saw a very hairy leg, and said, "That's not a people leg."

She lifted up the middle of the blanket, saw a very hairy arm, and said, "That's not a people arm."

She lifted up the top of the blanket, saw a very hairy face, and said, "That's not a people face. That is *not* my baby brother!"

"Now, Kristen," said her mother, "don't be jealous."

Then the baby reached up with its feet and grabbed her mother's ear and her father's ear, and they both yelled, "*Aaaaaahhhhhaaaaa!* It's a gorilla baby! We've got the wrong baby!"

"Let me do it," said Kristen.

So her mother and father put the gorilla baby on the chandelier in the living room, and Kristen went off to the zoo on her bicycle.

First Kristen looked in the snake cage.
No people babies.

Then Kristen looked in the wombat cage.
No people babies.

Then Kristen looked in the elephant cage.
No people babies.

Then she stopped and listened. From far away she heard, *"Waaa, waaa, waaa, waaa, waaa."*

"That's more like it!" said Kristen. She followed the sound. It was coming from the gorilla cage.

Kristen looked at the mommy gorilla and said, "Give me my baby brother." The gorilla jumped away and wouldn't give the baby back at all.

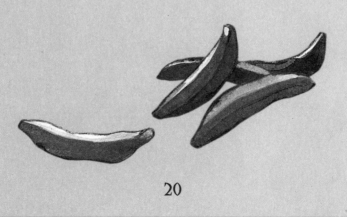

Then the people baby reached up and bit the gorilla on the nose, and the gorilla yelled, "*Aaaaaahhhhhaaaaa!*" and handed the baby to Kristen.

Kristen jumped on her bicycle and pedalled home.

Kristen knocked on the door: *blam, blam, blam, blam, blam.* When her parents opened it, she said, "Would you like to see your new baby?"

Kristen's mother lifted up the bottom of the blanket, and said, "Look, people legs."

She lifted up the middle of the blanket, and said, "Look, people hands."

She lifted up the top of the blanket, and said, "Look, a people face."

Kristen's mother picked up the baby and gave it a big hug. Her father took the baby and gave it a big hug. And her mother said, "Kristen, Kristen. You got the baby back. Good for you."

"But what are we going to do with all these other babies?" yelled Kristen's father. "There is a seal baby in the bathtub and an alligator baby in the fish tank and a gorilla baby hanging from the chandelier! We should take them back to the zoo."

But Kristen looked out the window and said . . .

"I don't think we'll have to do anything at all."

And everything was okay . . .
until Kristen's mother had twins.